Anthony Browne

# WILLY AND HUGH

Alfred A. Knopf • New York

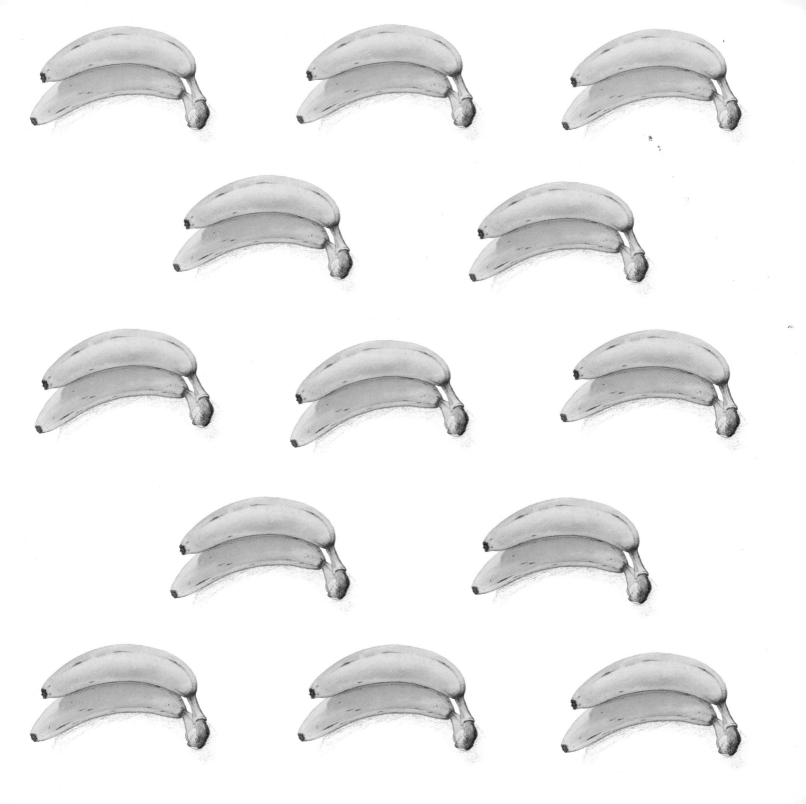

THIS IS A BORZOI BOOK PUBLISHED BY ALFRED A. KNOPF, INC.

Copyright © 1991 A. E. T. Browne & Partners
All rights reserved under International and Pan-American Copyright Conventions.
Published in the United States by Alfred A. Knopf, Inc., New York.
Distributed by Random House, Inc., New York.
Originally published in Great Britain by Julia MacRae Books.

First American Edition, 1991

Manufactured in Belgium
2  4  6  8  10  9  7  5  3  1

Library of Congress Cataloging-in-Publication Data
Browne, Anthony. Willy and Hugh/Anthony Browne.—1st American ed.  p.  cm.
Summary: Willy the chimpanzee is lonely until he meets Hugh Jape in the park,
and the two become friends.
ISBN 0-679-81446-9 (trade)   ISBN 0-679-91446-3 (lib. bdg.)
[1. Chimpanzees—Fiction.  2. Friendship—Fiction.]  I. Title. PZ7.B81984Wd  1991
[E]—dc20  90-4938  CIP  AC

Willy was lonely.

Everyone seemed to have friends.
Everyone except Willy.

No one let him join in any games;
they all said he was useless.

One day Willy was
walking in the park . . .

minding his own business . . .

and Hugh Jape was running.                    They met.

"Oh, I'm so sorry," said Hugh.

Willy was amazed. "But *I'm* sorry," he said. "I wasn't watching where I was going."

"No, it was *my* fault," said Hugh. "I wasn't looking where *I* was going. I'm sorry."

Hugh helped Willy to his feet.

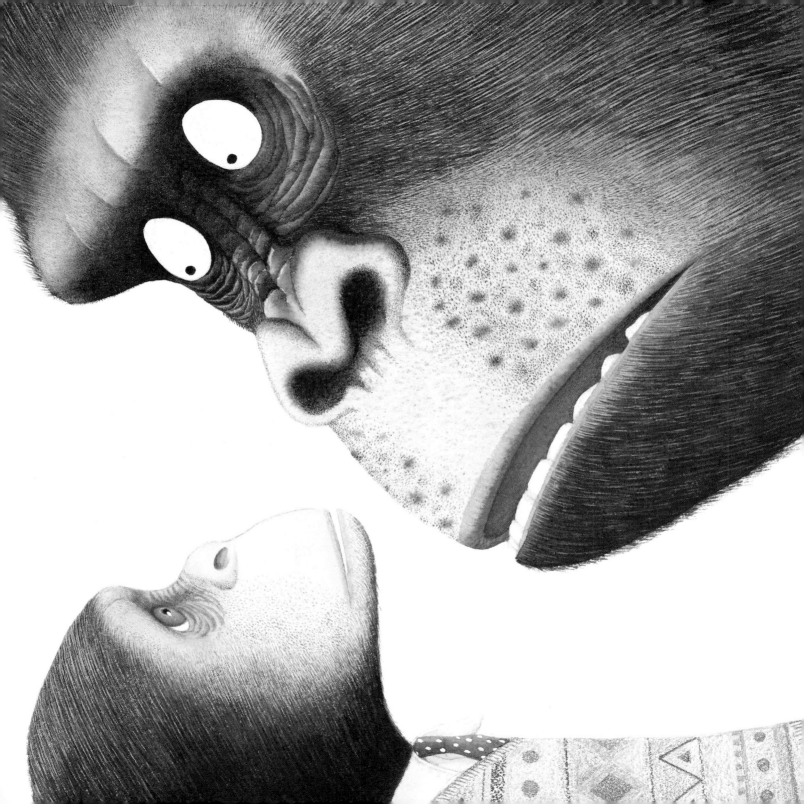

They sat down on a bench
and watched the joggers.
"Looks like they're *really*
enjoying themselves,"
said Hugh.
Willy laughed.

Buster Nose appeared. "I've been looking for you, little wimp," he sneered.

Hugh stood up. "Can *I* be of any help?" he asked.
Buster left. Very quickly.

So Willy and Hugh decided to go to the zoo.

Then they went
to the library, and
Willy read to Hugh.

As they were leaving the library,
Hugh stopped suddenly. . . .

He'd seen a TERRIFYING CREATURE!

"Can *I* be of any help?" asked Willy, and he carefully moved the spider out of the way.

Willy felt quite pleased with himself.

"Shall we meet again tomorrow?" asked Hugh.

"Yes, that would be great," said Willy.

And it was.

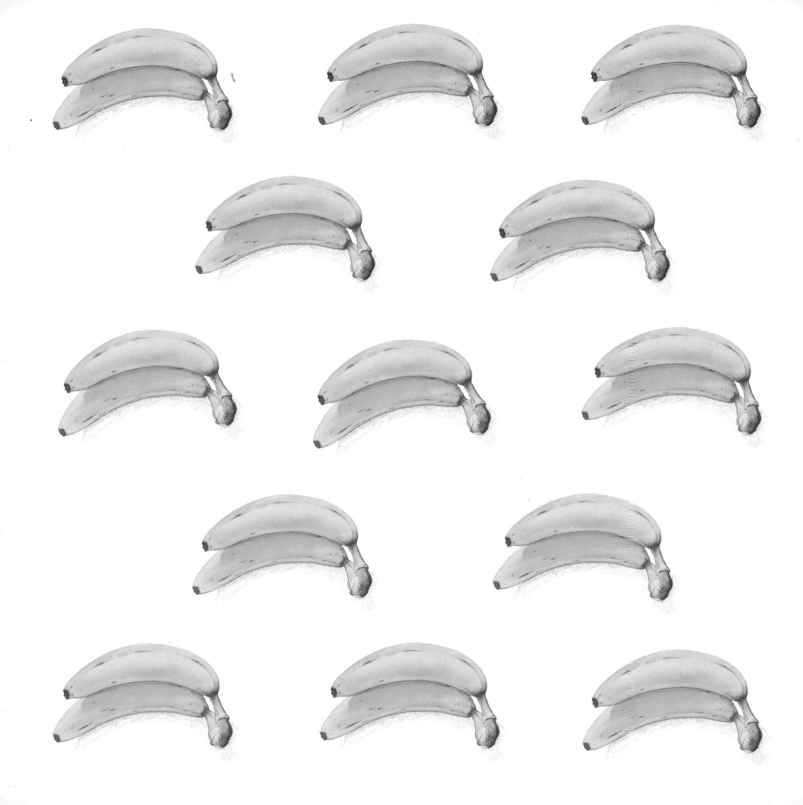